The Dog Poo Fairy

Tracey Bryant

For Phoebe and Hannah, my very own Fairies,
and my beautiful cat Fidget, always in my heart

Acknowledgements

For all your help, love and support, my partner Justin Turner, with the editing and grammar, I could not have written this book without you.

Also my great friend and talented artist, cartoonist, illustrator Ian D Johnstone for all your help. You are, so generous and I hope this book will give you the recognition you so richly deserve.

A big thank you to Helen Baggott who is an accredited proofreader and copy editor, thanks for all your knowledge and advice.

Many thanks to Wriggle my Burmese cat for keeping me company as lap warmer, attention seeker, coffee break companion and for walking across the keyboard.

1. Phoebe Bumble-Beebee

If fairies were in charge, the world would be a tidier place, don't you think? Your room would tidy itself when you weren't around, your homework would be done whilst you went out and all the washing up would magically wash itself whilst you still got all the pocket money. It's such a shame that you big people don't see many of them these days, and when you do it's pretty much always when no one else is around.

You are all very clever, I am sure, and know all about fairies with their peculiar ways, but allow me to enlighten you about where they go to school. The fairy school that's nearby, deep in the woods and not easily reached by big people is called 'The Academy for All Spells Great and Small'. It is in a particularly beautiful part of the countryside near where I live, off a canal path that borders a wide and green field full of lazy cows that can be seen eating their breakfast of grass and weeds first thing in the morning. I can't tell you exactly where the school is because they would have to move if lots of people turned up, as fairies like to be secretive around big people. I sometimes take a short cut home after I have been out all night and sit on the school lawn as the sun comes up. I watch as they fly to school and if I am lucky they bring me cake for my breakfast.

I was snoozing on the grass outside the school last week after eating a really rather delicious fairy cake given to me by a very pretty and friendly fairy by the name of Phoebe Bumble-Beebee.

She has beautiful long brown hair that almost covers her delicate silvery wings and is always the first to say good morning to me before fluttering off to class when the bell rings. She told me a very remarkable story last week and if you are quite ready, I will tell you all about it.

I'm not going to bore you explaining what a fairy school is, it's just like your school where you learn maths, English and all the other silly subjects. I've never been to school but Phoebe and Hannah Hollyhock (her best fairy friend forever) tells me the only difference is that fairies also learn how to use magic and cast spells.

Following a very dull maths lesson with Miss Belinda Bright-Spark, most of the class were on their Blueberry phones, U-phones or tablets browsing the Interweb. Don't be shocked, they have all the latest technology, just like you, and aren't all that different from you except they are small, have wings and can do magic spells when they feel like it.

Phoebe has a U-phone 7 which has a great camera for taking elfies (I think you call them selfies) and Hannah has a Blueberry phone, which is better for texting. They were both looking at the online shopping site for fairies called 'Glitter-R-Us', at all the cool new fairy glitter clothing that was on their wish lists.

"Have you seen these rainbow glitter leggings," whispered Hannah, showing her phone screen to Phoebe. "They are so cool; I am going to have to buy some."

"Yeah they are amazing, though I like the midnight purple ones better and they would look great with my silver moon T-shirt," replied Phoebe quietly, so as not to alert the attention of Miss Bright-Spark who was packing away her books and papers.

Phoebe was hovering over the 'Buy it Now' button when suddenly the door swung open and in bustled the busy Headmistress, Mrs Deirdre Dew-Dropper.

Not only does she drop dew on to all the flowers in the fields and forest, she also looks after the school and the pupils.

As she flew into the room she collided with Miss Bright-Spark who lost control of all her books and papers, scattering them over the floor. The whole class giggled as the maths teacher groped for her things around the feet of the Headmistress, who looked down at her with puzzlement on her face. Meanwhile, the sounds of bags being unzipped and chairs skidding on the floor could be heard as the whole class quickly hid their phones and tablets.

"Silence please, class," said Mrs Dew-Dropper in a raised musical voice. "Today I will be talking to you about careers." All the class moaned and started chattering. The Headmistress continued in a louder voice. "You are all in your last year and some of you will be going on to college or university, whilst some of you will not. I want you all to get into pairs and choose a career that you think would suit the other person. I also want you all to mix up; do not sit with your best friends as that would be too easy."

The whole class made a loud groaning noise and looked around, desperately trying not to catch the eye of anyone they really didn't like or want to pair up with.

"Come on, hurry up, everyone get out of your seats and move to a school friend you don't usually sit with," said Mrs Dew-Dropper ushering Miss Bright-Spark out of the class, who was still dropping the occasional paper.

Phoebe sighed as Hannah got up to find her second-best friend, Chloe Clover-Candy, who was a clever fairy but rather quiet. Everyone else moved like lightning to get to their next-best friends.

Things were beginning to look a bit desperate for Phoebe as the number of fairies left to pair up was looking rather small when she felt a hand grab her. Turning around she gulped. It was Kendra Splendour-Spencer, the school 'Know It All'.

Kendra has the most beautiful and wavy long blonde hair that glitters like gold in the sunlight. Her eyes are sky blue and they are so bright you can almost be hypnotised by them. She is the smartest fairy of the class and always comes top at every subject. All the other fairies are a little jealous of Kendra because she has so many stars to her name that she just sparkles. What is less attractive about her is that she is mean and looks down on those who are not in her fairy friend ring whilst making fun of them behind their wings.

Kendra has rich fairy parents who give her the most wonderful presents and fairy wishes, but she then comes into school bragging about them before throwing them away after a few days when she gets bored with them.

"Let's work together today," smiled Kendra. "I think we will get the best work done out of the whole class."

Phoebe's jaw dropped and she looked at Kendra wondering what on earth she could be up to. There was not a lot of choice left as they were the only two fairies not paired up. Kendra didn't wait for a reply and proudly sat down as Phoebe let out a long sigh.

Phoebe looked around the class, who were as stunned about what was happening as she was. Kendra began to get out her expensive gold pencil case as Mrs Dew-Dropper began to speak again.

"Class, I want you to write down in your exercise books what career would best suit your partner. I will look at them at the end of class and then plan next week's work experience for all of you."

"I can think of some wonderful jobs for you," whispered Kendra sarcastically.

Phoebe thought about what to put down for Kendra as she watched her scribbling at a frantic pace all manner of unpleasant and nasty careers.

Mrs Dew-Dropper walked up and down the classroom and boomed out, "Remember to write neatly in your exercise books, as I will be marking everyone's handwriting. You can also draw pictures if you like and I will give out extra stars for the best work."

Phoebe watched Kendra writing perfect swirls with a lovely gold glitter pen.

Mrs Dew-Dropper continued. "Just because you are fairies and can use magic, you still have to learn how to write neatly and not waste your spells on basic tasks."

As Phoebe sat chewing the end of her ordinary black biro, struggling to find inspiration, a career suddenly popped into her head that she knew would suit Kendra perfectly. Hannah's Uncle Bob works as a Dandelion

Fluff Sorter and he can talk forever about what his daily tasks involve and always mentions how the fluff gets up his nose. I happened to be near him one day when he was talking to Hannah. Bob just didn't shut up and I found my eyelids drooping and had a quick cat nap. Uncle Bob is one of the most boring people you could possibly meet so Phoebe thought the job must be really dull; the local newspaper always had loads of vacancies for fluff sorters, which is always a bad sign.

Kendra didn't like getting dirty and did not go outdoors if it was raining. Phoebe began to write down all the careers that entailed getting muddy, wet or working outdoors. She wrote down 'Tree Bark Grader', where you have to collect all the tree bark that has fallen off the trees and sort it into different tree types. Can you imagine how boring that must be?

Another idea popped into her head and she wrote down 'Cheese Hole Puncher'. This job may sound great to you if you like cheese, but think about all the cheese bits to clean up after you have made all the holes, not to mention the smell. Phoebe started to draw a picture of Kendra with cheese bits on the floor around her and bits of cheese in her hair. She was beginning to enjoy the lesson.

The school bell then rang and everyone got ready to hand in their exercise books. Phoebe was amazed at how the afternoon had flown by, like a fairy herding bees.

Kendra shot up from her chair and was the first to get to Mrs Dew-Dropper, who was tidying up the classroom. Hannah came quickly behind giving her best friend a tug on her wings as she walked past. "I'll see you outside," she said. Phoebe nodded and put away her things.

Outside the two friends flew slowly to the school gates.

"I am so excited about this work experience for next week," said Hannah.

"I'm not," said Phoebe worriedly. "I bet Kendra has picked some horrible jobs for me."

Hannah smiled, genuinely concerned and said, "I saw how quickly she grabbed you, and I bet that she has probably got a nasty little surprise planned for you, but I know you will get through it, you always do."

"Thanks, Hannah. What careers have you and Chloe chosen for each other?" Phoebe asked.

"I chose 'Caterpillar Cocoon Protector', 'Butterfly Herder', 'Bee Duster' and 'Grass Weaver'," Hannah said, counting them off on her fingers.

"Those sound much better than the things I am likely to get but let's go back to my house and I'll tell you what I chose for Kendra," said Phoebe. "We can also order those leggings we like, to cheer ourselves up."

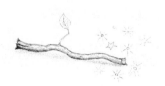

2. Work Experience Day

The weekend flew by like fairies racing on their school sports day. Monday morning dawned bright and clear and Mrs Dew-Dropper was out and about early on her way to school. Phoebe met up with Hannah, dreading the job she was going to have to do this week and as they flew into the classroom Kendra barged past them, giving a dirty flutter of her wings whilst making a beeline to her seat.

Phoebe tried to take her mind off things and noticed Hannah's new leggings.

"I love your new rainbow glitter leggings, they are so amazing," she said.

"Your new ones are pretty awesome too, the purple goes with your wings and they look good with your DFs," said Hannah. "Do you like my matching fairy dust pouch bag?"

Phoebe looked at the new pouch and remarked, "Yes, it's so cute and handy too; you can fit your phone into it."

I didn't know what DFs are because I don't wear boots, but Phoebe told me they are like your Dr Marten's boots but are called Doc Foster's. Why are they called that? Well, they are from the nursery rhyme whose first line is:

Doctor Foster went to Gloucester
in a shower of rain.

Can you guess what a fairy pouch is for? It is for fairy dust and is used to make big people and other things fly. It is harvested from mystical sources and I wish I knew where it was from as I think it might come in handy; all I can tell you is that it smells of chocolate.

"Let me take an elfie of us," said Hannah and she took her phone out of her new fairy dust pouch bag. "Say magic," she said taking a picture of them both, smiling.

"I'm nervous about today," said Phoebe. "I hope Kendra hasn't written a terrible list of jobs for me." Deep down she knew she had, looking across at Kendra's nasty smiling face beaming back.

Kendra threw a ball of paper in Phoebe's direction, which bounced and landed on the floor. Hannah picked it up and passed it to Phoebe who unscrewed the sheet of crumpled paper. She read:

> *Hi Phoebe, I think you are going to have a lovely time today, not!*

Phoebe thought quickly and wrote back on the reverse:

> *I hope you like your job too, it's perfect for you.*

She threw it back just in time as Mrs Dew-Dropper flew into class.

"Good morning, class; please settle down and put those phones away. Today I have organised everyone's work experience and I have chosen the jobs for each of you. I would like to say there were some very good and imaginative jobs to choose from, though some were a little over imaginative." Phoebe blushed as Mrs Dew-Dropper gave her a long and disapproving stare.

She continued, "The best overall writing and art work was from Kendra, with Phoebe coming second." Phoebe was amazed and Hannah nudged her in the side to say well done.

"I am going to call everyone up in turn to my desk and tell each one of you where you are working today. I will use my magic to send you to your workplace where there is a fairy supervisor waiting to train you in that particular job."

There were gasps of excitement from the class because it is very rare to have fairy magic cast on you from a skilled teacher like Mrs Dew-Dropper. Phoebe forgot for a moment about the horrible job she would likely be getting from Kendra and thought about the transportation magic; it would be so exciting.

"Kendra, would you like to come up to my desk first, as you were best in class," said Mrs Dew-Dropper.

Kendra got up smiling like the Cheshire cat (who, by the way, is one of my best friends). Kendra gave Phoebe a sly wink as she walked past, strutting her stuff and fluttering those wings way more than necessary to cover the short distance to where Mrs Dew-Dropper was sitting, list in hand.

All the class went quiet to hear Mrs Dew-Dropper.

"Kendra, I have chosen for you, trainee Dandelion Fluff Sorter."

Kendra gasped and her face went pale, her smile changing to one of shock. Looking back, she gave Phoebe an angry glare but the smile returned quickly when she remembered that the job she had suggested for Phoebe was much, much worse.

"Now is the time to cast the spell to transport you to where Bob the Dandelion Fluff Sorter works, he will be your supervisor," Mrs Dew-Dropper closed her eyes and chanted:

Come wind, come air; fly fast, be there!

Mrs Dew-Dropper threw some silver fairy dust from her pouch over Kendra, there was a sound like peas popping out of their shells and Kendra disappeared, with fairy dust falling out of the air where she had been hovering only a second earlier. It was beautiful silver glitter that glistened and sparkled as it fell to the class floor before it vanished from sight. The smell of chocolate filled the room.

You probably think that all fairies have wands. Well, that isn't true. If you are a highly skilled fairy you don't need a wand, you just use magic and can use your mind or voice to cast the spell; Mrs Dew-Dropper is one such fairy.

When the gasps and sighs from the class calmed down there was lots of excited chatting.

"Phoebe, would you like to come up now as you had the second-best piece of work in the class," said Mrs Dew-Dropper reaching back into her fairy pouch for more fairy dust.

She looked at Hannah with excitement and dread, who squeezed her hand. "You'll be fine," Hannah whispered.

Phoebe flew slowly up to where the smiling Mrs Dew-Dropper was waiting. "Phoebe, today you will be working as a trainee Tidy Hedgerow Fairy."

The words didn't go in straight away as Phoebe was expecting something far worse. She didn't know much about what a Tidy Hedgerow Fairy did but it didn't sound all that bad. She suddenly felt a bit ashamed that she had sent Kendra to boring Uncle Bob at the Dandelion Fluff Sorting Office.

Mrs Dew-Dropper continued, "I will now cast the spell to transport you to where the Chief Tidier of the Hedgerows will meet you, her name is Ellie Elderflower and she is a friend of mine."

Mrs Dew-Dropper closed her eyes and chanted the spell as before:

Come wind, come air; fly fast, be there!

Mrs Dew-Dropper threw some silver fairy dust over Phoebe who began to feel a tickling sensation travelling from her toes to the tips of her wings. Phoebe felt happiness and warmth spread throughout her body and thought this was like having the best present ever. The last thing she heard was a popping sound and the class disappeared from view.

Phoebe noticed she was suddenly outside, looking down at the school far below. She felt her wings open and a gentle warm wind blew her in the direction of the nearby wood. Phoebe was really enjoying the magic pushing her gently along like a soft fluffy cloud. It was so calming and relaxing that she later thought she must have fallen asleep for a moment.

When she next opened her eyes, a short time later, she was standing on the ground in the countryside, next to a tall and thick hedgerow.

3. The Chief Tidier of the Hedgerows

" Hello, Phoebe," said a voice behind her. "I hope you had a wonderful flight."

Phoebe turned round to see a rather plump fairy with a round kind face smiling at her.

"Are you Ellie Elderflower?" she replied.

"I am indeed, my lovely. Welcome to your first day in the Tidy Hedgerow department."

Phoebe gave her a big beaming smile, she was still feeling the effects of the amazing spell, but it also seemed the most natural thing to do on your first day in a new job. Phoebe's mother had once told her that if she didn't know what to do or what to say for any reason then it was better to say nothing and just smile. It didn't make you look more intelligent, but it made you look less like you were struggling to breathe.

Phoebe looked at the red-haired fairy in front of her, who was very tidy in her green uniform, which looked a bit tight in places.

"I know you will be feeling a bit light-headed from the flight and spell, so I have brought you some fairy cakes and dewberry juice," said Ellie, producing a small plate full of wonderfully colourful and tasty looking cakes. Out of a red tartan flask she was carrying, she carefully poured a cup of black dewberry juice and passed it to Phoebe, who was still smiling.

Dewberries are like blackberries but they start off purple and then ripen to black. They are found on small trailing brambles in hedgerows. Dewberry juice is really special, as it has fresh morning dew drops collected from flowers, funnily enough by Mrs Dew-Dropper.

The dew is mixed into the juice and it has the effect of making you feel less woozy after a magic spell, or simply if you have been up late and don't want to get up in the morning for school.

Phoebe drank the sweet and refreshing dewberry juice in one gulp and in an instant she felt wide awake and full of energy. Ellie then handed Phoebe a fairy cake. It had pink icing with rainbow coloured fairy wings on top that sparkled in the early morning light. It was so beautiful she didn't want to eat it, but at that moment Phoebe's tummy growled loudly, like a purring cat, and she knew it was time for a snack. Phoebe picked off the fairy wings and took a large bite of the cake. When she had finished the last piece of the cake she then delicately ate the fairy wings.

"Thank you very much," said Phoebe wiping her mouth with the back of her hand.

"You are most welcome," said Ellie putting away the flask. "Now it is time for me to teach you about hedgerow tidying."

Ellie told Phoebe about her responsibility to make sure there was no rubbish in the hedge or along the canal path. It seemed a very important job and she explained that if someone didn't tidy it up the rubbish left behind by the big people could harm the birds, mice, badgers, hedgehogs, foxes and other animals that lived nearby.

The poor animals would sometimes get caught up in the rubbish and hurt themselves and would also eat the plastic thinking it was fruit or berries, which made them feel very poorly.

"Plastic rubbish is the very worst kind of rubbish," said Ellie sadly. "It doesn't rot away and disappear nicely like natural things do. It causes a lot of harm to the countryside and looks very messy."

"That is terrible," said Phoebe. "But why don't the big people pick up their rubbish and take it home with them?"

"We don't know why," continued Ellie sadly. "We think some of them are just lazy or dirty and have no respect for the countryside. Not all the big people are like this and in some areas of England a Hedgerow Tidy Fairy isn't needed at all, though as you can see by looking at this hedgerow I am very much needed here. Having you here today, Phoebe, will be a great help."

Phoebe looked at the hedge and could see lots of colourful small plastic bags hanging on the branches with something dark in them.

"What are those hanging in the hedge?" asked Phoebe.

"Ahhh, those," said Ellie, with a knowing glance. "Those are dog baubles."

"Dog baubles?" said Phoebe. "I've never heard of those; are they like Christmas baubles that you hang on a tree?"

Just as Ellie was about to continue they saw a rather posh-looking lady in dark green wellington boots turn the corner ahead, walking towards them with a small brown and white dog on a lead.

Ellie beckoned Phoebe to the top of the hedge, whispering, "Watch this and find out how the dog baubles get made, I've seen this lady before and she always leaves one in the hedgerow."

There really wasn't any need to whisper or hide from the big people as they can't see a fairy unless they really truly believe in them, which is pretty rare these days.

Ellie continued to whisper just in case. "Oh yes, it's definitely her all right and that dog is ready to burst by the look of it."

"Burst?" giggled Phoebe.

"Shhh," said Ellie sharply, "the dog can hear us."

The lady was very nearly upon them and Phoebe could see that the dog was a fat brown and white Jack Russell. He was puffing and panting from the short bit of exercise along the path.

"Please stop, Mummy," barked the dog. "I need to go for a poo."

"Oh Mr Pickles," said the lady in a silly baby voice. "Do you need a plop-plop?"

Mr Pickles suddenly caught sight of the fairies and barked up to them.

"This is so embarrassing and I do apologise to you fairies. I am not a little baby and I wish she didn't speak to me like that. My owner is a bit stupid and she never understands what I am saying."

Animals can see fairies and fairies can speak animal languages, but they generally keep the secret from big people, who are too stupid to be able to understand either.

Mr Pickles was obviously desperate to go to the toilet.

"I'm sorry, fairies," said Mr Pickles, "but I really am going to have to go right here. I don't think I can walk another step."

"You aren't serious," said Phoebe covering her eyes. "I can't watch this, it will be gross."

"I will tell you when it is safe to look," said Ellie. "Unfortunately, it's all part of the job. You get used to it after a few years and you hardly ever notice the smell after a while."

Mr Pickles turned round and began to stoop, a look of pleasure and relief crossed the old dog's face. The lady looked away in disgust, got out her phone and started to text one of her posh friends.

"It smells horrible, has he finished yet?" said Phoebe still with her eyes closed.

Mr Pickles turned around mid-stoop with a worried look on his face. "Well excuse me, I am sure," he said rather crossly. "But what do you expect when she feeds me beef Wellington and leftover bits of bacon. I'd much rather have a nice bone, it would keep my insides a bit better."

The dog turned back and stood up, flicking the grass up several times with his hind legs.

"You can look now," said Ellie and Phoebe opened her eyes to see the lady put her phone away and take out a pink plastic bag.

"That's a big stinky one," said the lady screwing her face up and crouching down on one knee to scoop it up into the bag.

"Shout a bit louder will you," barked Mr Pickles, a look of embarrassment all over his wrinkled face. "I'm sure all the fairies in that wood over there would love to hear about it."

Phoebe watched as the young woman got back up, tying up the pink bag before walking over to the hedge and hanging it on one of the branches.

"I wish you wouldn't do that, it's so embarrassing and untidy," barked the dog.

"Awwhhh, are you are proud of your big ploppy, Mr Pickles? Well done, good boy," said the lady as she left the pink bag swinging amongst the hawthorn.

Mr Pickles looked up at the hedge and then at the fairies. "I am so sorry," he barked as his owner started to pull on his lead and they both walked away, Mr Pickles a lot lighter on his four old legs.

"So that's a dog bauble," said Phoebe sadly. "That is so disgusting, why do they hang it in the hedge?"

Ellie shrugged. "They think the fairies clean it up, which is actually the truth but they don't know that. They do not care about the countryside and all the animals in it. It is so upsetting and annoying to see them doing it and I've told Head Office that it is becoming a real problem here, we might even need to get a dragon out to scare the big people away for a while."

Ellie picked up a stick, flew over to a nearby bag and prodded it. "The bags don't rot or break down very easily so they would stay here forever if I didn't pick them up. That is why I need your help, and to ask you to come up with an idea to stop the big people doing this. Frankly, I've run out of ideas."

"Well it's not really what I thought I would be doing today," said Phoebe. "It is quite a dirty job, but I can see that it is damaging the countryside and becoming a real problem. I will help you and think of an idea to try and stop these lazy big people."

4. Jobbies

66 Well let's get started," said Ellie. "The first and most important thing is that you have your PPC."

"PPC?" said Phoebe, confused. "What's that?"

"It's your Protective Poo Clothing," chuckled Ellie. "I'm afraid it only comes in one size and doesn't fit very well, like most work clothing."

"Oh," said Phoebe blushing. "There seems to be a lot to learn on this job."

"Yes there is," said Ellie handing over a pair of pink Daisygold gloves, a pair of silver protective goggles and a pink apron. "Sometimes I forget how much I know and have to teach about cleaning up the countryside."

Phoebe started to put on the rubbery PPC and thought she must look a right idiot wearing it. She wished now that she hadn't worn her lovely new purple sparkling leggings and T-shirt.

As Phoebe put on her apron she noticed it had writing on it. On the top row it said *Trainee Tidy Hedgerow Fairy* and underneath in gold letters the motto of the department: *It's our job to clean up your jobbies.*

There was also a little gold picture of a dog bauble with a cross through it.

Phoebe looked down at it and thought that having *Dog Poo Fairy* on it would be more appropriate.

Ellie handed Phoebe a small notepad and pen. "I nearly forgot, this is your dog bauble notebook. I want you to record how many baubles you have collected today. Please let me know how many are tied to the hedge and how many you see on the floor."

The book had a purple glitter cover with *Dog Bauble Collection* written in gold letters. The pen was in a matching glittery purple, which was very pretty for such a yucky job.

"What do you do with all the bags?" asked Phoebe, worried she might have to pick them up.

"Before you start I will show you how to cast a spell to get rid of the bags. The first thing to do is to pick a branch off the hedgerow."

Ellie walked a little further along the path and spotted a good branch sticking out over the path. She snapped off a small part and handed it to Phoebe. "Repeat this spell after me," she said.

I pick this branch off the hedgerow tree,
To make a special wand for me,
Keep our countryside dog bauble free,
This fairy thanks you, hedgerow tree.

Phoebe then repeated the spell whilst holding the small branch. As she finished the last line she felt the wand wriggle in her hand, it felt warm and alive. The branch seemed ordinary enough and it didn't change shape or colour, but she knew it was now magical.

"Wow, that was awesome," said Phoebe.

"Yes," replied Ellie. "Nature has some wonderful magic in it, you know. Now bring one dog bauble to me and I will teach you the spell for making it disappear."

Phoebe flew over to the bag and reluctantly untied the bauble. She was glad she was wearing her Daisygold gloves as this wasn't a nice job at all.

You may be wondering how such a small fairy like Phoebe could carry such a large dog bauble. Phoebe told me that one of the first spells she learnt at school was how to shrink objects larger than herself. She said that it is so easy for her to do now and all she has to do is think of the object shrinking in her mind, touch the object and it shrinks to a manageable size. I told her that I hoped she didn't try to turn me into the size of a mouse because even though I do love mice I don't want to be that tiny. Phoebe reassured me that she could only change objects not animals, fairies or big people.

"Put the bag on the floor in front of me and then pass me your wand," said Ellie.

Phoebe put down the bag and handed her the wand. Closing her eyes Ellie began the spell:

> **Naughty human left you there,**
> **A dirty bauble without a care,**
> **So vanish now, into the air**
> **To keep the countryside clean and fair.**

As she spoke the last line, the bag disappeared with a loud plop and a shower of brown glitter fairy dust fell from the sky and disappeared into the ground without a trace.

"That was amazing," clapped Phoebe excitedly. "Will all the dog bauble bags just disappear into the air like that?"

"Yes, and nothing is harmed in the process," replied Ellie. "Do you want me to write down the spell for you or will you remember it?"

"No thank you, I will remember," said Phoebe nodding.

"Very good, my lovely," said Ellie. "I have to go to a meeting now, about targets and boring office stuff, but I will be back later. If you need me urgently remember to wave your wand in the air and say:

Elderflower, Elderflower fly to me,
I need your help, please come to me.

"Can you remember that too?" asked Ellie.

"Yep, I got it," answered Phoebe.

"Okay, see you later," said Ellie and vanished with a puff of gold glitter fairy dust that rained down and disappeared gently as it touched the soft ground. Phoebe stood all alone, looking at all the brightly coloured dog baubles hanging along the hedgerow. There were so many to deal with, she just hoped she wouldn't see anyone from school.

"Well, I guess I had better make a start," she sighed and opened her notebook.

5: The Disappearing Baubles

Phoebe flew over to a nearby blue bag tied to the lower branch of a beautiful patch of hawthorn in full bloom. As she pulled it from the branch there was a strong odour of very old doggie doo and she dropped it on the floor in disgust.

"This is going to be harder than it looks and smells," said Phoebe to herself.

Phoebe decided that she would place the dog baubles in one pile, count them all up and then she could make them all vanish later. She wandered along the hedgerow picking up all the bags and rubbish as she thought very hard about how to get the big people to stop leaving all the dog baubles. She was thinking so hard and putting the rubbish and bags on the large and growing pile that she sighed.

"I'll just pick up one more and then have a rest for five minutes."

She bent down to pick up one more bag that had been left next to the hedge and as she stood up and turned around she gasped in horror as she saw Kendra suddenly appear in front of her.

"Smile for the camera," said Kendra.

Phoebe, bag in hand, let out a shout, "Oh no!" and went bright red in the face.

"That's a great shot of you," said Kendra with a note of satisfaction in her voice. "I will put that on my Wingbook page for all the fairies to see." (Wingbook is the same as Facebook, but is just for fairies.)

"Please don't, Kendra, I look awful," exclaimed Phoebe.

"Too late, I already have," said Kendra with a nasty look on her face. "You just look a picture in your lovely work clothes. I am loving your new fashion."

Phoebe had forgotten that she was wearing a pair of silver protective goggles, pink Daisygold gloves and a pink apron. The picture would be seen by every fairy at school and Phoebe knew she would never hear the end of it.

Suddenly Kendra did an almighty sneeze. Phoebe looked at her and noticed she had a red rash all over her face and down her arms. Kendra's eyes and nose were also red and running.

"What happened to you?" said Phoebe, genuinely concerned.

"It's all your fault," said Kendra wiping her nose with a gold handkerchief. "You chose me to be a Dandelion Fluff Sorter, and I have come up in a rash."

Phoebe struggled to hold back a smile and started to feel a lot better; it was obvious Kendra wasn't enjoying her job either.

"I have been told by that boring Dandelion Fluff Sorter to come and help you, as I seem to be allergic to dandelion flowers," said Kendra.

Phoebe didn't think the day could get any worse, but she was a kind fairy and said, "I am so sorry that you have that horrible rash."

"You will be. And don't think that I will be helping you. I am going to sit and relax while I watch you work," said Kendra sitting down and crossing her arms defiantly.

Phoebe suddenly had an idea. "Kendra, you came at the right time. I was just going to cast my wonderful disappearing spell to get rid of the dog baubles."

"I bet you can't make them disappear, you are hopeless when it comes to magic spells," replied Kendra, now in full sulk.

"Of course I can, I have made some disappear already," lied Phoebe. "I have a very special wand that Ellie made and it really is quite wonderful at making things disappear."

Phoebe handed over the hedgerow wand to Kendra who looked it over before handing it back. "It's just a boring stick; there's nothing special about it," she snapped.

"It is special," repeated Phoebe. "It may not look like a posh wand but it works. Would you like to cast the spell for me?"

Kendra suddenly perked up and grabbed the wand back from Phoebe. "Okay but I'm not wearing that ridiculous uniform."

Phoebe beckoned Kendra over to where the large pile of dog baubles was laying.

"This looks disgusting, are those what I think they are?" said Kendra holding her pointed nose.

"They sure are," said Phoebe. "Now I'll tell you what to say to cast the spell." Kendra nodded waving the wand around like it was a conductor's baton.

"Point the wand at the pile of dog baubles and repeat the spell after me," said Phoebe.

> *Naughty human left you there,*
> *Dirty baubles without a care,*
> *So vanish now, explode in air,*
> *To keep the countryside clean and fair.*

Kendra quickly repeated the spell and suddenly there was an almighty loud bang and the dog bauble bags exploded all over the two of them.

Kendra was the first to scream. "It stinks! It stinks! I am going to be sick."

Phoebe quickly got out her phone from her fairy dust pouch bag. "Smile," said Phoebe as she took a picture of Kendra.

"You disgusting fairy!" screamed Kendra shaking with rage. "I will get you for this. You better not have posted that to Wingbook."

"Too late, I already have," said Phoebe with a little smile. She wanted to burst into laughter but didn't dare as she knew she looked a real mess too. Kendra's hair and face were dripping with dog poop. All Kendra's clothes were covered in it, there wasn't a piece of clothing on her that wasn't covered in the smelly mess.

"I am sorry, Kendra," said Phoebe. "The spell must have gone wrong, it didn't do that the last time I cast it."

Kendra, red with rage, threw a large handful of sweetly smelling gold fairy dust into the air and disappeared, leaving a smelly brown fog where she had been just a moment before.

Phoebe was rather glad Kendra had disappeared but realised she too was covered in the contents of the dog baubles and the smell was terrible. Luckily she had her Protective Poo Clothing on and had avoided the worst of the explosion.

Phoebe knew she was going to be in real trouble with Kendra but it suddenly gave her an idea. Just by changing one word in the spell it had altered the effects of the magic. She had added the word 'explode' and the baubles had done just that, instead of disappearing as before.

There was a lot of mess splattered along the hedge and grass and she thought she had better think of a spell to clear it up before anyone else came along. She pointed her hedgerow wand at the poop and cast the spell again:

> *I'm in a mess, dear hedgerow tree,*
> *Can you clean this poop for me?*
> *To keep this lovely hedgerow free,*
> *From all things that are untidy.*

The hedgerow wand began to twitch in her hand, but this time it felt much hotter. The wand cast out a bright light and in an instant all the mess had disappeared, as if it had never been there.

The whole hedgerow was nice and tidy again and Phoebe looked down at the brown stick in her hands, now cool once more. "Thank you, hedgerow wand," she said stroking the stick in her hands like a kitten. Resting it gently on the ground she took off her protective goggles and her apron, noticing for the first time how they were stained a very nasty and smelly shade of brown. Phoebe hardly dared to look down at her new leggings but was relieved to see they were still nice and clean.

She picked up the wand and was just about to fly over to the canal to wash her Daisygold gloves in the muddy water when she saw two dogs turn the corner and come sprinting head-long towards her, tongues lolling out of their mouths as they ran.

"Oh no!" sighed Phoebe. "Here we go again." And then she flew to the top of the hedge.

6: Banjo and Boone

The dogs bounded closer and then skidded to a halt in front of her. Phoebe noticed they were both brown and white Springer Spaniels and were busy sniffing all around the hedge. The larger of the two dogs had a brown marking that looked like a big patch over his left eye and he lifted his head up, sniffing the air. He barked at Phoebe.

"Oh hello up there, what's that smell? It seems to be coming from you. Is it a new perfume?" said the dog with the patch over his eye.

"It's a long story and I am covered in all sorts of smelly stuff," said Phoebe, not sure whether to come down from the safety of the hedge.

"You do look funny and a bit of a mess. My name is Banjo and my brother here is Boone." The other dog wagged his tail and gave a friendly little bark.

"Where's your owner?" said Phoebe.

Banjo looked over his shoulder. "Ah, he is so slow, he can never keep up with us but he will be here in a while."

"Do come down and tell us what happened," barked Boone, who had two brown markings over his eyes so that it made him look like he was wearing a mask.

"Okay, I'll give you the quick version of what happened," said Phoebe and she flew down next to the two dogs.

As Phoebe started to tell the story of the morning, Boone began to lick her.

Phoebe giggled. "Stop it, you are tickling me. You don't have to do that, it must be disgusting for you."

"I don't mind, I have cleaned worse," barked Boone who continued to gently lick Phoebe clean.

"Well I thank you all the same but now I really smell of dog," said Phoebe, feeling a lot better for being licked clean.

The two dogs lay down and Phoebe carried on with her story.

"So that's what has happened today. As you can see the dog baubles are becoming a problem in this hedgerow and I have to think of a way to stop the big people leaving them in this lovely countryside," said Phoebe.

"I hate that my owner hangs our jobbies in the hedge. It's so embarrassing leaving our mess for the other dogs to see," barked Boone.

"Me too," barked Banjo. "I hate having an untidy human who doesn't care for the countryside. We must try and make our owner see what he is doing and think of a way to stop him and all the other big people from doing the same."

In the distance Phoebe could see a man walking towards them. "Is that your owner over there?"

"Yes it is, here he comes," barked Boone.

"Well, I have been thinking of a magic spell that might help stop some of the dog baubles being left in the hedgerow," said Phoebe.

"Tell us quickly before he gets here," barked the dogs at the same time.

"This is the spell," said Phoebe, and she began to chant:

> *Help me again, old hedgerow tree,*
> *Baubles hanging next to thee,*
> *Make them take it home for me,*
> *And hang it in their...*

Phoebe paused. "What word rhymes with tree?"

Boone and Banjo looked at each other, thinking deeply.

"Pee?" barked Boone.

"Don't be silly," said Phoebe.

"I have a better word, lavatory!" barked Banjo.

"Hey, I know that word. That's where my owner goes to read a newspaper for a long time and sometimes he calls it a toilet," barked Boone.

"That's brilliant and it rhymes" said Phoebe. "This will be so good, if the spell works."

"Look, here comes our owner now," barked Boone and he turned around and ran to the tall young man with short dark hair.

"Do you think we can test this spell out?" said Phoebe to Banjo.

"Yes I think we should. I could do with having a number two anyway," barked Banjo.

"Come back here, Boone," barked Banjo. Boone was being stroked by the tall young man.

"Okay, I'm coming," barked Boone, and ran back to meet Banjo and Phoebe. "We both need to go for a number two, so we may as well test the magic spell out for Phoebe."

"I think I can squeeze one out," barked Boone. "All in the name of magic."

Phoebe looked away and flew back to the top of the hedge to wait. "Let me know when you're done and your owner starts to pick up your poop," she said.

Then the man caught up with them and said, "There you are, you two rascals; you shouldn't run off like that. I will have to put you back on your leads."

Banjo winked at Boone and they both began to squat.

"Oh, I see you are doing your business. I had better get some bags out of my pocket," said the young man.

"Please take the dog baubles home with you when you have picked them up," barked Boone at the man, but he couldn't understand Boone and all he could hear was barking.

"There's a good boy, Boone. You get so excited after you have done a poo, it's so funny," said the young man.

"No, I am not excited, I am trying to get you to understand me," barked Boone.

The man got out the bags and began to stoop.

"Phoebe, hurry, he is picking it up now," barked Banjo.

Phoebe turned around and flew down off the hedge next to where the man was just about to tie the dog bauble to a branch.

"I am going to wait till he has picked up the second one and then I will cast my spell," said Phoebe.

"I am sorry he is not taking them home with him," barked Banjo.

"That's okay. It's not your fault," said Phoebe.

The man finished tying the second dog bauble to the hedge and whistled to the two dogs.

"Come here, Boone, while I put your lead on you," said the young man. As he was putting the lead on Boone, Phoebe pointed her hedgerow wand at the two dog baubles and, raising her voice loud and clear, she chanted the spell she had just created:

> *Help me again, old hedgerow tree,*
> *Baubles hanging next to thee,*
> *Make them take it home for me,*
> *And hang it in their lavatory!*

Phoebe felt the wand buzz and wriggle in her hand again. There was a sound of 'pop' and 'plop' and the two dog baubles disappeared in a shower of brown glitter fairy dust.

"Wow, that was amazing," barked Boone and Banjo together as they sat watching. The owner was just putting the leads back on to their collars and didn't seem to notice what had just happened.

"I hope it has worked, but I won't know if it has. Only your human will know when he gets home if there are two dog baubles hanging in his lavatory," said Phoebe.

"Come on, Boone and Banjo, let's go home now," said the man pulling them away.

"If we see you again we will let you know," barked Boone as he was being pulled by his lead.

"Tell Ellie, the Head Hedgerow Fairy, when you next walk along here. She should be around here most days," shouted Phoebe as the dogs and their owner walked away from her.

"I hope it works and maybe it might stop him from leaving the dog baubles in the hedgerow," barked Boone.

"Nice meeting you too," shouted Phoebe. She watched the dogs walk away until they disappeared around the corner.

Phoebe was just wondering where Ellie might be when there was a loud ping and in a puff of gold glitter Ellie suddenly appeared in front of her. Phoebe nearly jumped out of her wings in shock. "Oh, you gave me quite a fright," said Phoebe.

"Sorry, I didn't mean to scare you," said Ellie laughing. "I can see you have been busy, the hedgerow looks nice and clean, but I can smell that not everything went according to plan. What have you been up to and where's your PPC?" asked Ellie.

"It's a long story, but I have picked up loads of dog baubles today. I have also come up with a spell to help stop the big people from leaving the dog baubles in or next to the hedgerow," said Phoebe proudly.

"It does look a lot tidier than this morning; you have been working hard. What is this new spell?" asked Ellie.

"Well, I pointed my hedgerow wand at two dog baubles that a big person had just tied to the hedge." Phoebe repeated the spell she had used on the bags just a moment before.

"Then the dog baubles vanished into the air, but I won't know if it has worked. The two Springer Spaniels that belonged to the big person said they would come back and tell you when they next come for their walk."

"It sounds like a good idea and the spell should work. I will try it out on the next person I see hanging the dog baubles in the hedgerow," said Ellie. "You have done good work today and I won't ask what else happened, as long as you didn't hurt anyone and everywhere is very clean and tidy."

Phoebe smiled to herself and she was just going to tell her about Kendra but thought better of it.

"You can go home in a moment but first please give me your wand, your Dog Bauble Collection notebook and your PPC," said Ellie politely.

Phoebe handed over the wand and notebook. "I just need to fly over and pick up the PPC. I should only be a second," she said. In a blink of an eye Phoebe had flown there and back with the dirty clothing that had saved her from all the mess earlier. "Sorry, it's a bit dirty," said Phoebe to Ellie.

Ellie looked at the work clothing. "I think you can keep them as a reminder of your hard work today."

"Oh thank you," said Phoebe with a confused look on her face. She wondered what she would ever do with them; perhaps boring Uncle Bob would have some ideas.

"Well, thank you again for all your hard work today. I will visit your school in the next two weeks to let you know how your spell has been working," said Ellie appreciatively. "If you would like a job when you have finished school I would be pleased to offer you the position as a Hedgerow Tidier, or perhaps we should call you the Dog Poo Fairy?" laughed Ellie.

"Thank you," said Phoebe, but secretly she thought she would rather be doing something else.

"Right, let's get you back home," said Ellie and closed her eyes ready to recite the transport spell to take Phoebe home again:

Come wind, come air; fly fast, be there!

The words had barely left her lips when she threw some gold fairy dust into the air and over Phoebe.

Phoebe felt the same tingling sensation again working its way up from her toes and up the strands of her hair. It really was an amazing sensation.

Ellie seemed to fade in front of her, as did the hedgerow and all the woodlands in the distance. Phoebe could feel her wings opening and a gentle warm wind was lifting her into the air. The sensation of being inside a soft fluffy cloud was so relaxing and as she gently travelled up and away from the ground she fell asleep.

In the next instant Phoebe was standing in her bedroom at home. "Wow! That was awesome," she said. "I feel so very relaxed but I must go and have a shower. I stink of doggy doo."

As Phoebe was brushing her long hair she wondered how Hannah had got on with her work experience today, thinking she would catch up with her on Wingbook and Flutter later. Flutter is the same as your Twitter social media.

Well, that is very nearly the end of my tale but I am guessing you would like to know if the spell really worked – and what happened with Banjo and Boone when they got home?

Well, I'll tell you.

7: What Happened Next

"Just let me wipe your paws before I let you into the house," said the young man, holding Boone's paw with a brown fluffy hand towel. "Your turn next, Banjo."

"I hate this bit, I wish he would stop it, it's tickling my paws," barked Banjo.

"Good boys, all done; you can both go in." The young man opened his front door and Banjo and Boone went running into the house.

"I need to go to the toilet myself now," said the young man speaking out loud to his dogs. He walked towards his downstairs toilet and as he went in he could see something colourful hanging inside.

"What on earth?!" he exclaimed. Hanging on the toilet flusher handle were two dog poo bags. The young man looked at them with a strange expression on his face. How did they get there? he wondered. They certainly looked like the bags he had foolishly left in the hedge only an hour ago.

The young man untied the dog baubles from the toilet handle and as he touched them he felt a tiny spark travel through his fingers and through his whole body to the top of his head. He suddenly saw an image in his mind of a fairy next to a hedge, looking very sad, holding a dog bauble and waving a naughty finger at him, it was odd because he could see she had midnight purple leggings on. The image vanished from his mind and he suddenly felt very sad too.

"What an idiot I have been," he said to himself. "It was just laziness hanging these bags in the hedge and littering the countryside. I suppose I thought that they would just disappear by magic, even though I know there is no such thing as a Dog Poo Fairy, I promise never to leave bags in the lovely countryside ever again."

And do you know, he was as good as his word and he never left a single dog bauble in any hedgerow, ever again.

So now you know the complete tale.

Phoebe never knew that her spell had an extra bit of magic in it. The magic was from her heart, from loving the countryside and wanting to keep it clean for all the animals and fairies.

This story is really important, so tell all your parents, brothers, sisters, nans, grandads, relatives and friends who have pet dogs.

Please do not leave dog baubles in the countryside, in hedges or anywhere else. There are very few Dog Poo Fairies in England and they can't clear them all up. It isn't a very nice job, as you found out by reading this book, so please take all your rubbish home with you and put it in your own bin, or the special bins you sometimes see along busy paths and parks.

The Dog Poo Fairies and the Tidier of the Hedgerow will be very grateful if you take them home with you and remember this saying:

Bin the dog baubles, don't hang them.

If you are lucky, and if you really care and love the countryside, one day you might be walking along a field with cows eating their breakfast of grass, near a canal path where lots of people and their dogs walk, and it might lead to a path in a large wood.

Somewhere deep in the wood, if you sit quietly, you might fall asleep, or you might stay awake and be lucky enough to have a fairy like Phoebe visit you. They might think you are good enough for them to show themselves to you if you believe in them, and they might say hello or show you some magic.

Now I must be going too, it's getting late and the sun has gone in and my owner will be calling me for my dinner. I think I have fish and crunchies tonight. If you haven't guessed already, I'm a cat, and I like to come here and listen to all the stories the fairies have to tell me. My name is Fidget and I am an orange tabby cat and if you see me on your walks say hello. Maybe give me a stroke if I am in the mood.

I might just put a good word in for you and you might get a visit from a fairy in midnight purple leggings.

The End

Lightning Source UK Ltd.
Milton Keynes UK
UKHW020207190119
335838UK00005B/78/P